KAREEM LEARNS TO COPE...
with Traumatic Loss

Antwan McKenzie-Plez

Illustrations by:
Daria Vinokurova

Book Designed By: MAS Studio
instagram.com/mas.designstudio

This book, my first ever, is intentionally and unapologetically dedicated to little Black boys all around the world who don't yet know the power of their vulnerability. Kareem's story is so many of our stories. The grief of growing up fatherless is a pain all too common in our communities. Give voice to your pain. It is safe to feel.

Kareem was angry.
He was angry with everyone, and everything.
Kareem seemed to be upset all the time.
He would yell, scream, cry, and protest every morning before school, telling his mom he just wanted to stay home with her.

At school, he was angry with his teachers and other adults... even his good friends.

He stopped caring about his grades at school and acted out in class all the time.

He even stopped participating in his favorite class, music.

He threw a lot of tantrums, more like a baby than the big mature 7 year old he is.

At home, things were not much better. He had trouble sleeping at night, felt nervous and afraid all of the time, and had a hard time concentrating and remembering things. He couldn't even focus on his chores or his favorite video games.

He sometimes felt all alone, even when there were lots of people around him.

Though he loved his mom very much, he sometimes said mean things to her. Of course, he would apologize because he didn't really mean the things he said, but sometimes he felt he couldn't control it.

Kareem was angry... and it only got worse with time. Kareem's anger started shortly after the terrible thing happened to him and his family.

Their whole lives changed about a month ago, when Kareem's father died.

Last month, Kareem's dad left for work and never came back home.

Later that day, a police officer knocked on the door and asked to speak with Kareem's mom.

Kareem heard mom scream, "No!", and then began to cry. Mom then told Kareem the worst news he had ever heard in his life.

On that terrible day, Kareem learned that his father had been attacked by someone while at work, and that he did not survive.

Kareem had so many feelings after this terrible day, that it was hard for him to understand them all.

Then, the anger started. The anger felt much easier to feel than all of those other confusing feelings and emotions... so he chose to stick with anger.

It started out really tiny, but then it grew bigger and bigger every day.

He even became mean towards his very best friend, Jaden. Not everyone at school knew about the terrible thing that had happened, but Jaden knew. So Jaden was patient with Kareem, and tried his best not to take his anger personally...

but Jaden became worried as time went on and things got worse.

One day, Jaden asked Kareem if he wanted to talk.

"Talk about what?", Kareem said.

"Well", replied Jaden, "we can talk about whatever you want, but I was wondering if you wanted to talk about the anger. Like, why have you been so angry lately? Is it because of your Dad?"

"I don't want to talk about that!", shouted Kareem, "You wouldn't understand anyway!"

Jaden calmly said to Kareem, "'Reem, you're right. I don't know what it feels like to lose my Dad, but I do know what it feels like to lose someone I love in a scary way."

Curious, Kareem asked, "You do?"

"Yes, I do", replied Jaden, "but I will not talk about it if you still don't want to talk."

"I guess that would be okay", said Kareem.

"Okay", Jaden continued, "Well, my grandpa died about two years ago because he got Coronavirus. It was like, one day he was happy and healthy, and then the next day he was so sick and couldn't breathe on his own. One day, he went to the hospital... and never came back home."

Kareem paused for a moment to think about what Jaden had shared. Then he said, "Wow. That's really sad. It sounds like almost the same thing that happened with my Dad. He went to work one day, just like always, and then I never saw him alive again. Someone... killed him." Hearing himself say those words, Kareem began to feel tears well up in his eyes. Taking another moment to think and breathe, Kareem asked, "Were you close to your Grandpa?"

"Oh yes!", replied Jaden, "We were the very best of friends. We did a lot of cool things together, like fishing, playing board games, and talking about all sorts of cool things he had done in his life. My grandpa was cool... and I loved him so much."

"I feel that way about my Dad. He... was my best friend, too", said Kareem.

Kareem continued, "Now, I just don't know what to do. I just feel like nothing in the world makes sense anymore. The world doesn't feel safe and I'm afraid all the time."

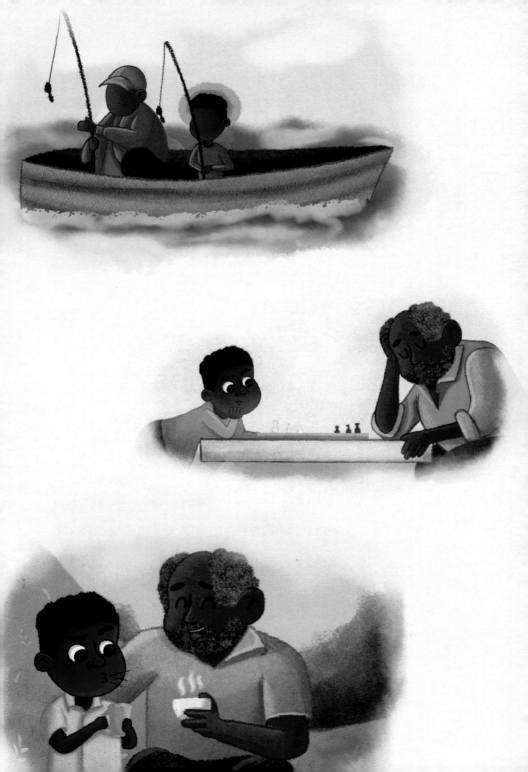

Jaden shared, "I felt that way too, for a long time. That's what happens when someone we love dies in such a bad way. It's so hard to feel safe again, but I promise you that feeling will eventually go away if you keep talking about it." Kareem began to cry.

"See! This is why I don't want to talk about it! Every time I think about my Dad being taken away from me, I cry and then I can't stop it. I HATE talking about this!", Kareem screamed.

Jaden held Kareem's hand and said, "'Reem, it's okay to cry. I cried for a really long time when my Grandpa died. You just go ahead and cry. I'll be right here to sit with you."

"But what if I can't stop?", asked Kareem.

"I asked my therapist the same thing. He told me that even though it felt like I would never stop crying, eventually I would... and he was right, 'Reem", Jaden reassured him.

In between sobs, Kareem asked, "You have a therapist? What's that?"

Jaden explained, "Yes, I have a therapist. A therapist is an adult who knows how to help kids who are having a hard time. My therapist's name is Mr. Malik. My mom took me to see him after Grandpa died and I've been meeting with him every Tuesday since then. He helps me to talk about my feelings and he also helps me to understand my feelings a little better. Mr. Malik really helped me to feel better about what happened to my Grandpa.""Did he teach you how to stop crying every time you think about it?", asked Kareem.

"In a way", Jaden explained. "He taught me that it's important to let myself feel the sadness instead of trying to ignore it. Ignoring the sadness and trying to force myself not to think about it only made things worse. He taught me that if I let myself think about and feel the feelings, I would feel much better afterward. 'Reem... he was right. That's why I'm telling you that its okay for you to cry. Just let it out."

Wiping his tears away, Kareem replied, "I do feel a little bit better now."

Jaden hugged Kareem, "It's okay Main Man. I'm here for you whenever you want to talk... or cry."

"I just don't want to be soft... you know what I mean?", asked Kareem. "Yeah, I know what you mean", replied Jaden, "but another thing Mr. Malik taught me is that having feelings does not make you soft, and crying takes more bravery than pretending like you're not hurting, because crying means that you are facing your fears and pain instead of running away from them. Facing our grief is the only way to get better."

"Really? I guess that makes sense...but what is grief?", asked Kareem.

"Grief", explained Jaden, "is how we feel after someone we love dies. It's all of those big feelings that you feel about losing your Dad... and that I still feel sometimes about losing Grandpa."

Confused, Kareem replied, "Oh, I see... but wait, I thought you said Mr. Malik helped you get over your... grief. Why do you still feel the big feelings about your Grandpa?"

"It's kind of hard to understand", replied Jaden, "but grief is not something that just goes away."

"But if it never goes away, then what's the point of doing all of that talking about it and feeling those yucky feelings?", asked Kareem.

Jaden smiled, "Talking about it and letting yourself have those feelings won't make the grief go away, but it will make the feelings and memories easier to handle. Mr. Malik says that the grief is just a reminder of all of the love we have in our heart for the person who died. If we wish the grief away, it would be like wishing our love away, and we don't ever want to do that. We don't want to just forget about the people we love, right?"

Pondering, Kareem replied, "Hmmm... I guess that's right. Jay, you're pretty smart about this... grief stuff. Maybe I should try going to therapy, too."
"Yeah, you should ask your mom about it. It is really helping me and my family", said Jaden.

Excitedly, Kareem replied, "I will. Our talk is already making me feel better. Is there anything else you could tell me to help me out, for when I'm feeling this way again?"
Reaching into his backpack, Jaden replied, "Actually...

Mr. Malik gave me this to help with my grief when those feelings come up." Jaden pulled out his personalized "My Grief" Journal for Kids: A guided journal for processing traumatic loss and showed Kareem all of the cool and helpful journaling exercises he could use to begin to feel better.

He showed Kareem how he could get a copy of his own and also gave him the link to Mr. Malik's website to show Mom so that Kareem could give therapy a try for himself.

Kareem thanked Jaden for being such a great friend. And so began Kareem's healing journey.

ABOUT THE AUTHOR:

Born and raised in Miami, FL, Antwan McKenzie-Plez A.K.A. "Twan the Counselor" is a proud South Floridian who is committed to serving the needs of the most marginalized in his local community, and now the global community through mental health education.

Antwan is a Licensed Mental Health Counselor, with National certification. He is also a Certified Grief Professional. His private practice, located in Fort Lauderdale, FL, is named Its All Grief, LLC. Through his practice he works as a specialist in treating trauma and grief through groundbreaking techniques including EMDR, Cognitive Processing Therapy, Trauma-Focused CBT, and Brainspotting. He specializes in treating pre-teens, adolescents, and adults with issues related to grief, trauma, PTSD, stress management, anxiety, depression, life transitions, and is LGBTQIA+ proficient. Antwan is also considered an expert on issues related Neurodevelopmental Disabilities, including Autism Spectrum Disorder, due to his 15+ years of training and experience working with this population. He is a self-proclaimed "Neuroscience Nerd" with a love for the human brain and it's natural capacity to access true healing. He calls himself, "a counselor by profession, but a healer by calling".

Antwan also co-owns Able to Dream, Inc., a Social Services Agency with his partner Daniel. The agency specializes in providing mental health counseling and direct care services to children and adults with Intellectual and Developmental Disabilities- another population he is passionate about and has dedicated most of his career to serving. They operate a nonprofit organization with the same mission.

Antwan's professional credentials include a Bachelor of Science in ESE Education K-12, a Master of Arts in Clinical Mental Health Counseling, a Graduate certification in Alcohol & Drug Abuse Counseling, certification as a Certified Grief Professional, Certified Autism Spectrum Clinical Specialist, and certifications in Integrated Medicine as well as Dialectical Behavior Therapy. As of the writing of this bio, Antwan is also in the process of becoming a Master Certified Addictions Professional and pursuing board certification as a Board Certified Behavior Analyst.

Antwan lives in the beautiful and vibrant city of Fort Lauderdale, Florida with his husband and partner of over 15 years, Daniel. They are adoring uncles to Ace, Craig, Nehemiah, Kenyodda, Gustavo, Kiley, Caedence, Ca'loni, & Ahmir.

They are also doting Godfathers to Nicholas, and dog dads to Paris & Dash.

You can learn more about Antwan's work by visiting www.itsallgrief.com

Made in the USA
Columbia, SC
18 March 2022

57687110R00029